MAMA does the MAMBO

STORY BY
KATHERINE LEINER

MA
BO

ILLUSTRATED BY
EDEL RODRIGUEZ

HYPERION BOOKS FOR CHILDREN
NEW YORK

Many thanks to my Monday Morning Comrades:
Janie Furse, Bette Glenn, Marilyn Kaye, Anne Adams Lang, Joanne McFarland, Gretta
Sabinson, Lavinia Plonka, and Michele Willens. Marylee Gowland for her eye to detail.
And finally, my wonderful editor, Maureen Sullivan,
who directed me with the lightest touch, like an angel. —K.L.

Special thanks to Jim McMullan for his generosity and guidance
and to my wife Jennifer for her endless support. —E.R.

For information address

Hyperion Books for Children,

114 Fifth Avenue, New York, New York 10011-5690.

First Edition

1 3 5 7 9 10 8 6 4 2

Printed in Hong Kong

The artwork was prepared using pastel, gouache, and spray paint on colored

papers with monoprinted woodblock ink linework.

LIBRARY OF CONGRESS CATALOGING-IN-PUBLICATION DATA

Leiner, Katherine.

Mama does the mambo / Katherine Leiner; illustrated by Edel Rodriguez

p.   cm.

Summary: Following the death of her papa, Sofia fears that her mama will never find

another dancing partner for Carnival.

ISBN 0-7868-0646-X (trade)

[1. Dancing—Fiction. 2. Grief—Fiction. 3. Cuba—Fiction.]

I. Rodriguez, Edel, ill.   II. Title.   PZ7.L5346 Mam 2001

[Fic]—dc21   99-86584

Visit www.hyperionchildrensbooks.com

To Makenna Goodman — K.L.

Para Mima, Pipo, Abuela, Tía Nancy, Samid y Liset — E.R.

After Papa died, Mama stopped dancing. Just like that, he died, and just like that, the dancing in our house stopped. Of course, how could it not. There was no one in our house for Mama to dance with.

Sometimes, I thought I missed Mama's dancing more than I
missed Papa. I know for sure I missed the music. But mostly
I missed the way Mama danced everywhere:

while she cooked our dinner,

while she hung the laundry,

while she swept the courtyard,

and even while she shopped.

At the end of a long day when Papa got home from sugar harvest, I loved the way Mama looked at him as he came toward her with his quiet, hushed, almost whispered, "let's dance."

The record player was always on at night. I missed the deep, hollow hit of the first conga that caused Papa to snap his fingers and got Mama's shoulders moving in one direction and her hips in a whole other.

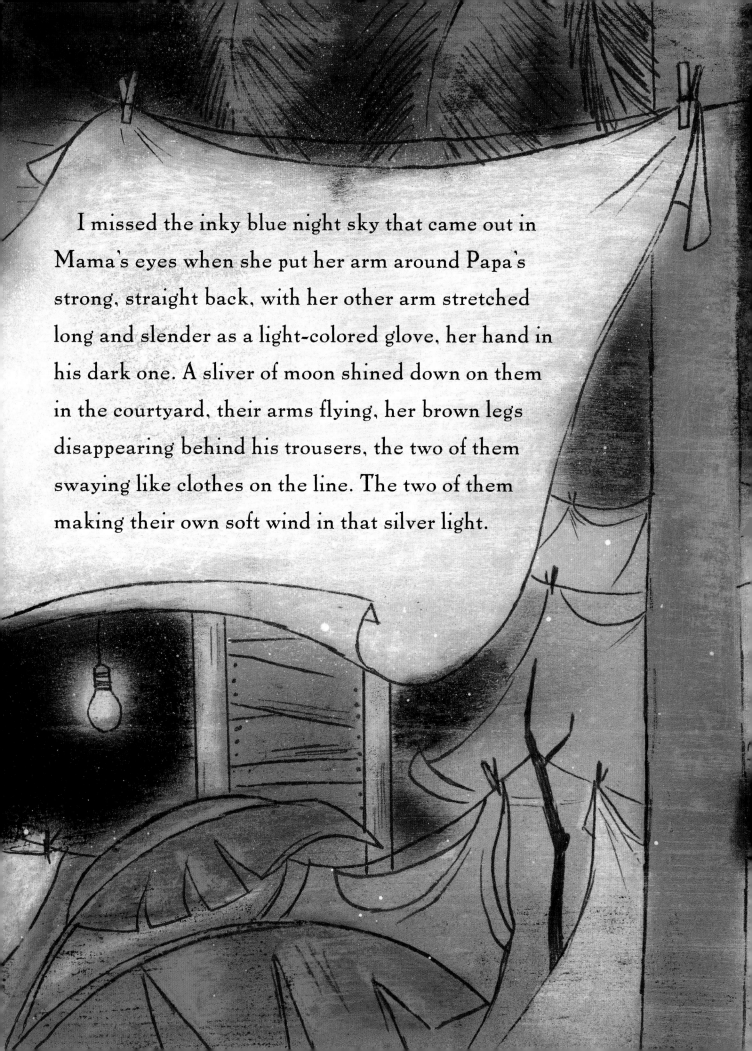

I missed the inky blue night sky that came out in
Mama's eyes when she put her arm around Papa's
strong, straight back, with her other arm stretched
long and slender as a light-colored glove, her hand in
his dark one. A sliver of moon shined down on them
in the courtyard, their arms flying, her brown legs
disappearing behind his trousers, the two of them
swaying like clothes on the line. The two of them
making their own soft wind in that silver light.

Papa held the beat, and Mama, the rhythm.
The sound of their hands when they came
together was like palm leaves flapping in the wind:
Mama's against Papa's, Papa's against Mama's; her
crimson skirts whipping a million lights, Papa like
the sparrows in the tamarind tree, the two of them
their own hurricane.

On Carnival morning, Mama wore
layers of gauze skirts and her ruffled
blouse settled just off her smooth
shoulders. Papa's brilliantined hair was
slicked shiny as a mallard's feathered
back. I wanted to look at them forever.
But Papa slipped out front to puff on a
fat cigar. Mama said he was always
nervous before they danced. She wasn't.
She turned on the toes of her
black-patent high heels,
around and around, giving
me a long last look at her.

Afterward, everyone came by to say how grand they'd been,
Mama and Papa

doing the merengue,

the tango,

the rumba,

and the chachacha.

But Mama always smiled and said, "I love the mambo best."

One spring has already come and gone. Carnival's almost here again. When I see Marina, who lives next door and is pulling her laundry off the line, she tells me, "Sofia, your mama needs *un compañero para bailar el mambo.*"

Un compañero? A partner? I cannot imagine anyone but Papa dancing with Mama.

Then Rosa, who cooks in the fancy *paladar* in Miramar, says, "*Chiquita Sofia, es importante* to find someone who can sweep your beautiful mama off her feet. *Ha llegado la hora.* It is time!"

Rosa tells Mirna, who runs the projector at Cine La Rampa in Vedado. And Mirna tells Dori, who sings boleros at the Casa de la Trouva in Centro Havana. All of them agree that Mama needs a partner; it is time. But who? Who will dance with her? Is there anyone who can dance the mambo with Mama? I am so nervous, my arms and legs shake like the beans in the maracas.

Perhaps I am worried for nothing. Because people come from all over Havana. It seems everyone wants to dance with Mama. Selvagio from *el mercado*, Esdras from *la farmacía*, Pablo from *la oficina de correos*, and Miguel in his shiny red Chevrolet. They all come to the courtyard.

"Sofia, Sofia," Mama's friends coo at me like excited pigeons gathering on the high stone wall. "See. See how many there are to choose from." They point at the long line of possible partners for Mama. All I can think of is Papa.

Soon the air is filled with the squealy strains of the fiddle and the bright jingle and shake of the maracas. Someone plays the conga. Mama smiles, but her heart is not in it. Her skirts stay in the closet, her feet, bare.

Eduardo comes, too. He brings melons and cuts them in bright juicy pieces for our guests. He brings *malangas* and cooks them till they are soft and mixes them with butter till they are sweet. He brings lamb and we shred and cook the meat and eat *ropa vieja*.

Mama laughs when Eduardo tells a joke. Mama smiles when he asks her what she wants for dinner.

"*Eduardo es muy simpático.*" Rosa thinks Eduardo is so nice.

"*Eduardo es muy guapo.*" Dora thinks he is so cute.

Eduardo takes us to La Habana Vieja
and we sip coconut milk straight from the
nut with thick straws. He takes us out for
long walks along El Malecón, the waves
breaking over the old stone wall.

"*Tu mamá quiere a Eduardo?*" Marina wants to know if Mama likes Eduardo.

Of course Mama likes him. We both like Eduardo.

But Carnival is six days away. "*Concentración, Mamá!*" I remind her that Eduardo can't dance.

One quiet night when Eduardo comes by, he seems different. Perhaps he is taller? Is that possible? On his head, his straw boater seems to tilt just right and his clean, white *guayabera* makes his dark eyes glow.

His shiny black shoes are made for dancing. I hold my breath, hoping against hope. But when the music starts, long and slow, tuning itself up to the mambo, Eduardo's feet seem put on backward. He tries to dip Mama, but her back is taut as the royal palms that dot El Malecón. Mama tries to twirl, but Eduardo is off the beat. Even before the song is over, he breaks away to check the *arroz con pollo*.

While Eduardo sets the table, I fill in. I put my arm around Mama's back, holding her firmly. I reach for her other hand. I remember the steps that Papa stepped. As we warm to the music, I dip her low and deep. "Mama, this will never do. It's two days till Carnival and Eduardo still can't dance."

The next day, Eduardo comes by with a basket full of fruit: *plátanos*, *papayas*, and a *piña*. We cut them up while he tells me his latest fishing story. I like his smile, from ear to ear. We scoop black beans for dinner and he shows me how to soak them. He teaches me how to play checkers. Before lunch, he takes his clarinet out of his bike basket and plays a sonata.

"Let's practice!" I remind them, clapping my hands. I turn the record player up loud. Eduardo trips over Mama's feet. She trips over his.

"Everyone's expecting you to dance," I tell her. I glare at Eduardo. I point at Mama. "You need a real partner!"

Mama smiles and shrugs and touches Eduardo's face.

On the day of Carnival, the streets are filled with banners: red and green and blue. A million people all dressed up like bougainvillea and orchids. The air smells of *limas* and gardenias. Mama has on her red dress and high-heeled black dancing shoes. Her thick, dark hair is pulled back in a barrette and behind her right ear is a white hibiscus flower.

Eduardo looks nice. He has on a crisp, clean, white jacket. The creases down his *pantalones* make his legs look long and graceful. He is holding Mama's hand firmly. Unfortunately, that doesn't mean he'll be able to dance.

I have on a pile of Mama's skirts and my own new, tight, white blouse settled just off my shoulders.

In the Plaza de la Catedral there is a rumba playing. Mama and Eduardo watch the other dancers. Then the band plays a fast chachacha. Mama and Eduardo clap their hands. When the merengue plays, Mama and Eduardo start to sway.

Finally the conga player hammers out the beats and the fiddler picks the first strains of the mambo. I hold my breath. I feel the crowd holding theirs. We are all looking at Mama. Mama smiles at Eduardo.

But then she stretches out her hand and motions for me to join her. I am confused as I walk across the crowded area to the dance floor. Everyone is quiet. Mama's eyes shine like two bright moons. She puts her arm around my straight, strong back. Her other arm, long and slender, stretches out to meet my own dark hand. As she dips me back, we look at each other, and I smile up at her.

Our skirts whirl around us and I am lost in the motion, lost in the wind of our dance. Mama holds the beat and I am the rhythm. And there, in front of all of Havana, I am dancing with Mama, and Mama is dancing the mambo again.

GLOSSARY

arroz con pollo: rice and chicken

boleros: love songs

la farmacía: the pharmacy

guayabera: traditional embroidered shirt

limas: limes

malangas: vegetable similar to a potato, with a turniplike flavor

el mercado: the market

la oficina de correos: the post office

paladar: home-style restaurant

pantalones: pants

papayas: tropical yellow fruit

piña: pineapple

plátanos: bananas

ropa vieja: shredded meat stew